ENSŌ

| A CONNECTION OF FABLES |

BY MICHAEL BAILEY

ILLUSTRATED BY L.A. SPOONER

PUBLISHED BY WRITTEN BACKWARDS

WWW.NETTIRW.COM

LIMITED EDITION

ISBN-10: 1461136652
ISBN-13: 978.1461136651

THIS SIGNED NUMBERED EDITION OF ENSŌ
IS LIMTED TO 100 COPIES

THIS IS # __2__ OF 100

MICHAEL BAILEY

ENSŌ

TABLE OF CONTENTS

THE LONG SLEEP OF CATERPILLARS

Two caterpillars once grew up together, one green with yellow stripes, and the other yellow with green stripes, both the size of a finger. The color of their skin didn't matter much to their friendship. They were inseparable.

"What do you want to be when you hatch from your cocoon?" said the yellow.

"I don't know," said the green, "but I hope I'm beautiful."

Beauty can be an ugly word sometimes.

"Not me. I don't care if I'm beautiful," said the yellow. "As long as I have wings and can fly away, that's all that matters to me. My wings can be black and ugly."

"Don't you want to attract a handsome boy moth? Handsome boy moths look for beautiful girl moths, and if you're black and ugly, no one will want you."

"Not true," said the yellow. "Some caterpillars like black and ugly."

"I hope so," said the green, "because my parents were like that. I don't want to grow up to be like them. I want to transform into a beautiful moth with vibrant colors. Orange, I hope, or maybe shades of yellow, like you."

The two caterpillars shared the maple leaf. Both knew they had to fill their stomachs to prepare for the long sleep.

"Do you think it hurts?" asked the green.

"You should never be afraid of pain. Pain's temporary and lets you know you're alive. The more pain you go through when you're younger, the more complex your wingspan will be when you're older. I hope it hurts a lot."

"Me too."

The yellow caterpillar inched along next to the green. Neither led. Both took turns, not necessarily following one another, but simply remaining companions on their journey through the impending change. They were stronger together.

"Over here," said the green, venturing wayward beneath the shade of a fallen branch.

"There's not a lot of food over there," said the yellow. "There's still some left—"

"Trust me."

"Okay."

The yellow caterpillar with the green stripes followed her friend this time. The fallen branch held two small maple leaves: one a lively green, the other a dried yellow.

"Hey, just like us," said the yellow.

"Quiet," said the green, crawling on top of her matching leaf.

The yellow caterpillar joined to feast but was stopped as her green friend arched, rearing onto her back legs in a threatening manner.

"Go to the yellow leaf," she said.

"We need to prepare," said the yellow. "That one's wilted."

"Trust me," she said again.

"Why won't you share?"

"We're not here to eat," said the green. "Stay still and not another word."

"It's not fair!"

The green caterpillar reared again and twisted her body to knock the yellow caterpillar onto the wilted leaf. Nutrients remained in the veins, green-striped like her, but the blade was not worth the struggle.

"I'm sorry," said the green. "Be quiet and still."

A bird-shaped silhouette emerged and the yellow caterpillar with the green stripes understood. Sometimes preparing for the future meant not doing anything at all, such as innocently lying in wait while a not-so-innocent world carried on.

Survival is important for becoming something new.

The brown finch landed next to the fallen branch with its monstrous shadow blocking the sun. The winged giant hopped around the leaves, looking for food, pecking between pebbles and twigs in the dirt.

The green and yellow caterpillars were invisible to the bird, camouflaged against their similarly-colored leaves.

A second finch landed, chirping, followed by a third, their heads cocking from side to side as they fed on marching ants. With the last of the ants eaten, the birds flew away, leaving the caterpillars safe once again.

"Thank you," said the yellow.

"You would have done the same for me," said the green.

"Yeah."

The caterpillars fed until their bellies filled and the bright orb in the sky fell beneath the horizon. They had traveled nearly across the plane of grass to a white picket fence next to an old oak. Both would burrow underground by the roots on the other side of the tree where they would begin the transformation.

"Are you ready to pupate?" asked the yellow.

"I think so, but I'm scared."

During adolescence, both had discussed when and where they would build their cocoons. Neither knew how to construct the protective shell, or even how to dig, but they'd figure it out together. How difficult could holometabolism be?

"We'll do it together," said the yellow.

"Promise?"

"Even if it hurts."

Near the fence, they came to a silk bridge.

"What is it?" asked the green.

"I don't know."

"Looks like a shortcut to me."

The silk bridge led directly across a deep, dark gorge in their path. Taking the bridge offered more time to solve the pupa dilemma.

"Let's take the long route," said the yellow.

"It looks strong enough to cross," said the green.

"I think we should continue the way we were going."

"Trust me."

The same trust had saved her life from the birds.

"Come on," said the green. "I'll go first to make sure it's safe."

The green caterpillar stepped onto the silk. She struggled with her footing, but managed to crawl out a ways.

"It's sticky," she said, "but strong enough to hold us both."

The yellow caterpillar watched her friend

crawl halfway across, and then tested the silk. She had sixteen legs: six thoracic or true legs bunched at the front of her body, eight abdominal prolegs, and two larger legs in the back. With all sixteen fighting the tackiness of the bridge, it would take much effort to cross.

She had her true legs secured when the silk rope shook.

The green caterpillar writhed, her body flagellating.

"What's wrong?" asked the yellow caterpillar, but her friend was silent, the segments of her body wriggling, mandibles chattering wordlessly.

A shiny black creature pounced onto her friend from out of nowhere, biting into her, its long forelegs hitting her body, hitting her face, pushing her as she fought, and then it scurried effortlessly out of sight.

"What is it?"

As the green caterpillar squirmed, the long-legged creature fell onto her again, pincers sinking deep. Her green friend flailed, falling onto her side, sticking against the silk. The next bite made her still. The attacker relaxed, slowly circling around and then on top of her. Long black legs held an equally black body high into the air to reveal a red splotch on its belly.

She had never seen anything like this before, but the red warned of evil.

The silk vibrated as the yellow caterpillar pulled free, as if she had plucked one of the strings. This caused the creature to step off her friend for a moment and advance, but then it returned to its kill, wanting nothing to do with her.

The yellow caterpillar could only crawl away in a slow escape.

"I'm sorry," she said. "I should have gone first. I should have led. We should have taken the longer path."

She mourned her friend and would have to figure out holometabolism on her own.

"I'm so sorry."

She crawled the long way around, avoiding the shadowy gorge, to the other side of the tree.

Underneath the cover of the thickest branches, she burrowed under the moonlight.

The yellow caterpillar found comfort as she spotted her friend, encased in a cocoon, nearly camouflage against the white silken bridge. Her friend was on her way to transformation.

The shiny black creature had returned to the shadows.

"We will fly together soon."

No longer alone, the yellow caterpillar with green stripes nestled underground, where she shed the last of her skin to reveal her cocoon, which would offer protection while her body broke down into undifferentiated imaginal cells to reform and shape a beautiful moth.

THE FOX AND
THE FIELD MOUSE

1

"You are alone, aren't you?"

The field mouse looked around cautiously. He wasn't much afraid of spiders in general, but this one, this kind, with the shiny black body and bright red splotch on its belly, sent shivers down his back. They *were* loners, for the most part, but many loners in a concentrated area could be trouble.

"I guess if you had friends, I'd be dead already."

It wasn't such a nice thing to say, even to a spider. He felt bad for saying it. He thought of apologizing, but the damage was done and the spider charged across her web, those eight legs surprisingly fast.

She had caught him off-guard. The field mouse nearly tumbled backward off the fence-post. Agile, the field mouse somehow managed to escape, quickly turning and darting across the white painted wood, hopping to the trunk of a nearby oak tree, and back to safety.

Was that a spiny leg that had brushed my tail?

He thought so. He had nearly brushed death.

Never again would he take that shortcut to the gardens. Likewise, he would never take the shortest path to the gardens, which ran parallel to the woodpile, where such vile creatures like this shiny black spider lurked. He saw them some-times, hiding in the many shadows.

"Stay away from the pile," his friends had warned.

He'd gone there once, after a hard rain, like the one the night before. The wild mushrooms were plentiful around the base of the pile, often growing directly on the wood. He hadn't seen the spiders, then, but knew they were there, the same way he knew stars still filled the sky when the sun rose and turned the world above light blue. The same stars, every night. Rain had washed away the spiders' webs and they'd rebuild, he knew. And sometimes they hid, like the stars, waiting for the sun to go down. Without the sun, shadows were no longer shadows and their hiding places opened up to the rest of the world.

That thought scared the field mouse more than anything at all.

2

The garden was abundant with life.

Various lettuces filled one box, carrots in another, along with the usual tomatoes, beans, squash and a few fruits. The garden was filled with moving life as well. Bees pollenated the flowers, a hummingbird stuck its proboscis into a hanging feeder filled with red sugar water, beetles and ants roamed the box tops, and the air buzzed with insects and chirped with birds. Freshly watered by the rain, a few of the planter boxes had soil tunneled by worms.

The orange and white pup drew the field mouse's attention, however. Never before had he seen such a strange-looking creature.

He thought of it as a pup because he or she seemed young and dog-like, yet had cat-like features, such as the pointed ears that stood straight up, and the bottlebrush tail. It dug its nose into the corner of a planter box on the opposite side of the garden.

A cat surely wouldn't do such a thing.

Quietly, the field mouse edged along the base of the nearest box. Curiosity called for a closer look.

A brown nose rose from the soil and turned his direction. Marble eyes saw him.

The field mouse froze.

A cat would properly pursue, head low to the ground, eyes never leaving its target. A cat would slowly stalk him, ears, back and tail completely flat, one paw slowly moving in front of the other.

A cat would glide across the ground in this slowest of motions until close enough to pounce. He had watched a few of his friends go this way to the great beyond.

The orange and white pup, however, surely an adolescent, by the look of him, paid no further attention. The nose buried once again into the soil, prodding, and returned with a small potato wedged in its mouth.

The field mouse unfroze.

A cat would never eat a potato.

The foreign voice of a human called out across the yard and the orange and white pup fled.

3

When he returned home to the nest in the field, the mouse forgot to mention the sighting of the pup in the garden. His mind was preoccupied with baby arachnids.

"I think we should move to another field,"

said the field mouse, "or at least farther into the field. I don't want to risk the lives of our children."

The mother of three mice snarled a bit, her whiskers furrowing beneath the pink dot of her nose. "But we've moved three times already," she said. "We seem to be distancing ourselves from food."

"We'll find more food," he said.

"Running away from our problems is not always the best solution," she said. "Sometimes we need to face them."

The field mouse thought of the path to the garden. The shortest route ran along the woodpile of shadows and through the white picket fence by the oak.

"I'll help protect the family, Daddy," said his youngest. She showed a defensive stance.

"Me too," said her brother, doing the same.

"You will do no such thing," said their mother, pushing a piece of carrot to their third child.

"I just want for all of you to be safe," said the

field mouse, "and well fed. If we decide to stay here—"

"We're staying here," said the mother.

"Like I was saying, if we decide to stay here, we need to abide by a few rules. And this goes for all of you, even me. No exceptions."

The family of field mice quickly ate, intrigued.

"No woodpile."

"But the mushrooms—" his youngest said.

"Soon the woodpile will be overrun. It will no longer be safe. It's not safe now. We will have to find mushrooms elsewhere. I can begin my search tomorrow. I know how you all love mushrooms. But, no woodpile means no shortcut to the garden."

"Please tell me we haven't lost the garden," said the mother.

"We still have the garden," he said.

This caused a great sigh of relief.

"It's a long path around the house, I know, but it's a safe path. Who knows? Maybe I'll find us a nice patch of mushrooms along the way."

All three of the children brightened.

"No playing by the oak tree."

"There's a lot of oak trees, Daddy," said his daughter.

"No playing by the oak tree by the white picket fence. Nearest the house. The one with the cracked trunk where the squirrels are always stashing their finds."

"There's lots of other oak trees, Daddy."

4

The field mouse didn't mean to exclude the pup sighting in his family's morning discussion. He had merely forgotten, distracted perhaps by his fear of the spiders. He had forgotten all about him until later that afternoon when he explored the long way around the house to the garden.

Part of an orange and white tail poked out of a tangle of wild blackberry bushes running along a small creek.

Potatoes and berries: such a strange diet for

such a strange-looking creature.

Silently, the field mouse followed the creek until he skirted his 'safe distance' with the pup. The tail was motionless. He watched long enough to determine that the pup had most likely fallen asleep while eating the wild blackberries.

"Pup?" said the field mouse, and he waited.

The bottlebrush was still.

Cats wouldn't eat potatoes. Cats wouldn't eat berries. But cats *would* stay motionless, for what seemed lifetimes, before they pounced. This creature surely wasn't feline, and if he or she were readying to pounce, it would pounce in the opposite direction of the tail, which now pointed straight at the field mouse, for he had slowly crept closer to investigate.

"Pup?" he repeated.

He was no longer a 'safe distance' away and was certain he could be heard.

The tail lay motionless.

Upon closer inspection, this wasn't even the same pup. The tail was larger, darker, aged.

Creatures that ate potatoes and berries surely didn't eat mice. This thought ran through his mind over and over again as he approached.

"Hello?"

Even if it were sleeping, the field mouse was sure his voice would be heard and the creature would startle awake.

Yet the tail remained still.

Something was wrong.

The smell told him this, as well as the inedible fungi that had sprouted around the fallen creature. Mushrooms only ever grew on things that were no longer living. And the white larvae, like ever-bending grains of rice, only ever fed on things that were no longer living.

5

He continued his exploratory journey around the house. The long path to the garden took three times longer than the shortcut past the woodpile, yet it was much safer. Instead of the typical shadow cover, the sun warmed his travels, and it was comforting. The sun seemed to rid the world of vile creatures.

"Hey, you're new," chirped a finch.

"Not new, really," said the field mouse.

"Haven't seen you before. Seed!" The finch, with its yellow beak, pecked the ground. "Nope. Rock."

The bird hopped along the ground next to him, pecking, shaking her head, pecking.

"Seed! Nope. Piece of wood. Where you headed?"

"I'm on my way to the garden."

"Where you from?"

"My family and I live near the rosebushes on the other side of the house."

"Roses by the oak?"

The finch hopped, pecked.

Nearly everything she picked up in her beak, she shook back out. She followed alongside him.

If they were ambushed by a cat, at least the cat would go after the much distracted bird first, though the field mouse wouldn't wish such a fate on any creature. It was a horrible thought and he felt bad for even thinking it.

With exception to the wings, they were about the same size.

The finch was so distracted, in fact, that she didn't even notice he hadn't answered her question about where he lived. He lived by the red roses, but didn't tell her this.

"Seed! Yep, seed."

"Have you ever seen an orange and white cat that isn't really a cat? Big, bushy tail, with ears as tall as you and me?"

"Cat here's gray and black striped," said the finch." She pecked the ground a half dozen more times before saying, "Only cat I've seen. Does it yip?"

"I'm not sure. The one I saw dug for potatoes in the garden." He decided not to mention the one he'd found by the wild blackberry bushes.

"Potatoes?" The bird snatched a twig, shook it free, and kept hunting. "Not a cat. Fox. You saw a fox."

"What's a fox?"

"Not a cat."

"Thanks," said the field mouse. The bird wasn't much to talk to, but he felt safer having her there.

"Caterpillars!"

The finch flew off and landed next to a few birds that looked just like her.

When the field mouse finally made it to the

garden, the fox pup wasn't there as he'd expected. He wondered if the pup knew about the dead fox in the wild blackberry bushes.

Perhaps they were related. How could the pup react to seeing such a thing? Perhaps the pup was lost, alone, scared...

6

The distance between the nest by the rosebush and the garden was going to be a problem.

Three times the distance meant three times the amount of time it took to get from one place to the other, and three times the effort to move food from the other to the one place.

It took most of the day to move a carrot, a bundle of strawberries and a stack of peapods.

"I don't see how this is going to work," he said to his family. "We need to move to the other side of the house."

"I like it here," said their oldest child.

"Me too," said the next.

"Me too," said the next.

"And our family is only getting bigger," said the mother. "A few more are on the way. We're in no condition to just pack up and move. Any luck finding mushrooms?"

The field mouse thought of the dead fox.

"None that are edible."

The children seemed disappointed.

"I can help look tomorrow," said his oldest, although she was far too young still to scavenge.

The field mouse thought of the fox pup digging for potatoes on its own, perhaps too young to scavenge.

"Maybe she can go with you tomorrow," said the mother.

He thought it over.

Together they could move twice the food. If only the boys were older, they could all go out and bring in four times the amount of food in the same amount of time.

Toward the end of summer they'd be old enough to scavenge as a pack.

"Tomorrow you can come with me," he said to his daughter.

"I don't want to go," she said, "but I agree with Daddy. We should move. Not to the other side of the house, though. We're field mice. We should be in the field."

"Absolutely not," said the mother.

"We *have* relied on the garden more than we should," he said. "The garden won't always be here. It's gone every autumn, and stays gone through winter, and not until late spring each year do we get to live in this paradise."

The family sat idle, pondering the idea.

"After the babies come," said the mother, "and only after they're old enough to move safely.

"We can all work hard over the next few months. We'll pack as much food as we can and will store it here. We'll move only when we're absolutely ready to move.

The youngest two didn't seem to care.

The oldest seemed excited.

The mother looked concerned.

Later that night, when the children were fast asleep, he asked her if she had ever heard of a fox.

"Orange and white, you say?"

"With ears like ours."

"The size of a cat?"

"But not a cat."

"Do they eat mice?"

"This one didn't want to eat me."

He told her about the potato.

"I think he may be an orphan."

7

The pup was there late the next morning. The garden was once again alive with life. Instead of digging for potatoes, the orange and white fox bit into an unripe, green tomato and pulled it free from the branch. With his head low, he ate.

"I like your taste in food," said the field mouse.

The young fox rose from the ground, startled, and took another bite. "What if I liked eating field mice," he said.

"Do you?"

"Nah, I'm messing with you. Others might, but I stick to vegetables. If it has legs or talks, I won't eat it."

The fox ate the rest of the unripe tomato.

"You should try those when they're red," said the field mouse.

"I've only ever had them like this."

"First season here?"

"I don't know what a season is, but we've only ever seen green ones. We've only been here a few days. I don't think we're supposed to be here, though, because the thing that lives in there scares us away."

His nose pointed to the house.

"You keep saying *we* and *us*," said the field mouse. "Where's the rest of your pack?"

"The last time the thing with the scary voice came out, he came out with a dog. My mom and brother were on one side of this place and I was on the other. The dog chased them one direction and I went another."

"Where are they now?"

If foxes could shrug, this one shrugged.

"I don't know. My mom always said that if we ever get split up, or lost from one another, that we should meet here, by these boxes. We got split up three days ago. Maybe they got so lost they forgot their way back here."

The field mouse somehow knew the aged tail he had seen poking from the wild blackberry bushes belonged to this poor creature's mother.

His brother, if the dog didn't catch him, too, was most likely lost and alone like this pup.

"I'll help you find your family," said the field mouse. "I'm good at following tracks."

"Mom always said to meet here if we ever get lost."

"I have an idea. If you help me bring a bunch of food back to my place for my family, I will help you find *your* family. We can make trips from here to there all day, so if they return to the garden, you'll see them. If by the end of the day you don't, then you can meet me back here in the morning and together we can try to find them."

"You promise you'll help me find them?" the fox asked.

"I promise."

8

Seven trips back and forth between the garden and the nest by the red rosebush yielded enough food for weeks.

The fox taught the field mouse about reburying the root plants—the potatoes, carrots and beets—to make them last.

This was something he had never thought of before. Basically, transplanting the vegetables.

"That's why I dig roots so much," said the fox. It was a clever pun.

He was a fast digger and did most of the work.

"Just watch for moles," he said. "They'll steal your food without you even knowing it.

The mother was hesitant at first to let the fox into their home, but after seeing how willing he was to help and how gentle he was around the children, she quickly grew fond of him.

"What does your mother look like?" she asked. "How will the two of you find her?"

The fox did the shrug thing again and said, "She looks like me, I guess, but her tail has a black spot on the very tip."

At those words, the field mouse's heart sank. The tail poking out from the blackberry bushes had a black mark on the tip. He must not have hidden the apathy well, because the fox's expression saddened.

"You've seen her," he said.

The field mouse nodded.

"And my brother... did you see him as well?"

The field mouse shook his head.

"We'll look for him in the morning. You can stay here tonight."

And that was the last they spoke of the long sleep.

9

The fox led him to the edge of the garden to the place where he had lost track of his family.

They took the shortest route, which meant passing the woodpile and then the white picket fence by the oak tree, an area of the farm now flourishing with spiders. With the fox at his side, however, the field mouse felt safe and the spiders hid in the shadows.

"Here," said the fox. "The three of us were here when the door opened and the dog started the chase. I ran that direction," he said, pointing to the east with his snout, "and my mom and brother ran that way."

His snout turned to the west, toward the open field where the field mice had earlier discussed moving their home.

Even after several days, the tracks were still

visible. Heavy paw marks chased smaller, faint paw marks from the past, which they followed into a present field of tall grass and shrubs. A few matchstick trees spiked the sky.

They happened upon a hollowed out stump.

"This is where the chase split."

A single, smaller set of tracks led toward a gathering of manzanita. A larger set of tracks, trampled upon by a heavier set of dog tracks, most assuredly, led to what the field mouse could only believe would be the wild blackberry bushes that ran along the creek bed.

"Your brother went this way."

The fox sniffed the ground, turned his head, and looked the direction of his mother. At this level, the fox and the field mouse were the same height, and for the first time they were eye to eye.

"Do you really think he's still alive?" said the fox. "It's been three days and—"

"You and your brother are the same age?"

"Yes."

"Well, it's been three days and *you're* still alive.

Alone, you've found a way. And there are no tracks that follow his into the field. Alone, he has also probably found a way."

With this new hope, the fox sat upright, towering over the field mouse. The warm sun shimmered yellow off his orange coat of fur. His ears perked at the distant sound of a dog back from the opposite direction, but he seemed unafraid.

10

Along the way, the manzanita slowly overtook the field. The farther they ventured, the less the sun's heat bore down on them. The creek had somehow wound back around to join them. It was much cooler, the ground damp and soft.

"Mushrooms!" exclaimed the field mouse.

They sprouted everywhere around the flaky, brown and red branches of the manzanita.

Grabbing a mushroom cap with both paws, he took a generous bite.

"Are they good?" the fox said.

"*Are* they good," the field mouse replied, not as a question.

The fox sniffed suspiciously before taking a bite.

"Well?"

"Delicious."

"I can see why your brother chose this direction. Me and my family could *live* out here. We seriously could and just might. This is paradise."

"Brother?" said the fox, looking around.

"This way," said the field mouse.

The tracks ended at the creek, but he could see that they started up again on the other side.

Rocks large enough to hold his weight worked as a dry bridge to cross the water. Seven hops and he was across. The fox leapt over the entire thing in a single bound, his back feet splashing in the water at the edge.

Together, they followed the tracks as they appeared and disappeared in the dirt, until they ended completely at a hole dug into a mound. The field mouse was about to ask what it was, thinking of course of snakes and other nuisances in the wild, when the fox told him.

"It's a fox hole."

The black mouth in the ground looked ready to swallow them both.

"Brother?"

Scurrying from within the mouth caused soil to rain from its dirty lips.

The field mouse hunkered behind the hind

legs of the fox, ready for the worst of things imaginable: the head of a large snake to emerge, or the legs of a hairy tarantula, or perhaps some kind of ground-dwelling owl.

Instead, a black nose poked out, followed by a white and orange snout speckled brown from burrowing in the fox hole for who knows how long. The fox's brother sprung from the hole. Without the dirt, the two would look nearly identical.

They brushed noses and danced playfully around each other, the field mouse backing away carefully to avoid getting trampled.

"He got Mom," said the dirty fox.

The brother must have found her on its own, such a horrible thought. Images of the aged fox tail filled the mouse's mind, along with thoughts of the dog...

"I know," said the clean fox. "My new friend told me." He motioned to the field mouse. "He helped me find you. He has a family, too."

"Thank you," said the dirty fox. He turned to

his brother. "I got lost and couldn't find my way back to the place Mom told us to go if we ever got lost."

"We can live here now," said the clean fox. "You can, too," he said to his new friend.

11

"There are mushrooms everywhere," the field mouse said to his family later that evening. "And running water, and places to hide, and fewer things to hide *from*. The foxes said they'd help us with a root garden. What do you say?"

THE DEATH
MOTH

A moth once emerged from her cocoon after being drowned by a morning rain. Water seeped into the soil around her home, softening the outer shell. The scab-red case split as tiny legs poked through, introducing her dark world to light. She chirped through the struggle, but eventually freed all six of her legs from the pupal exoskeleton and rose out of her dirt grave.

"You have a face on your back," a voice in the oak tree said, "a gray face."

The moth, exhausted from her transformation, simply listened.

"I saw a dead cat once in a field and the face on your back looks like the dead cat's face. A skull, they call it. You have a skull on your back."

"What colors am I?" the moth said.

"Besides the face, you're darker than the mud around you, like a starless night."

"No colors at all?"

"None that I can see, but your wings aren't ready yet. You need to let them stretch a while. Maybe you should perch up here, let them breathe."

The moth with the skull on her back shook the dirt and crawled toward the trunk of the giant oak. She traveled the exposed roots, hazy from the long sleep, skittering in zigzag paths.

"You're a strange looking bird," said the voice above.

Do birds eat moths? she wondered, remembering the finches when she and her friend were still in caterpillar form, how they eagerly pecked at the ground searching for food, for things that wriggled. She wanted to ask if the voice in the tree was that of a bird, but if a moth asked a bird such a thing, it would draw suspicion.

"I'm unique," the moth said.

"What were you doing in the mud?"

"Sleeping."

"You're not a bird, then. Can you fly?"

"Not yet. My wings are wet."

"Don't worry, I won't eat you. Moths are too powdery. No, I prefer worms and caterpillars."

The moth didn't want to tell this potential bird that she had not yet learned to fly, and that before her long sleep, she was wriggly food to the mammal. Instead, she kept her wings back to cover her caterpillar-like body. At the trunk, she climbed, claws hooking into the bark, and her wings slowly opened.

"I knew you were a moth."

The moth chirped, ever so quietly, wings stretching a little more.

"Birds can't climb, not like that, and you're smaller than most birds I've seen. Big for a moth, though."

"I used to be a caterpillar."

"But you've transformed. You have wings now."

"Does that change who I am?"

"It changes everything. We're nearly the same. Why did you chirp?"

"I was scared, thought maybe you'd consider me a bird again."

While climbing the bark, the moth's eyesight slowly improved, her dizzying walk steadying as she adjusted to her new body.

Walking was much easier when she had more legs. Six didn't seem enough, and the new ones were so much longer.

"Besides, how can a bird eat something with wings?"

She recognized the fuzzy outline of not a bird, but an orange butterfly.

"You're a monarch."

"I led you to believe I was a bird because I thought you might be a bird."

"Have you seen my friend?" she said to the butterfly.

"What does she look like?"

The moth looked for the white cocoon of her friend on the silk bridge, but the cocoon and the bridge were both gone, perhaps washed away by the rain. A new, different bridge filled its place. Maybe she had already hatched and flown away, unable to find where her friend had burrowed.

"I'm not sure. Similar to me, perhaps."

"Then no, I haven't seen her. You have some color under your wings."

"I do?"

"Yellow. And stripes on your back, too, like a bee. Your forewings are mostly black and brown like bark, but I think your second set of wings may have some yellow. Stretch them out."

The black and yellow moth extended her reach, exposing her hindwings. With her new eyesight, her peripheral vision extended far beyond what she was used to seeing. The hindwings were almost completely yellow, but she could not extend them far.

She was nearly to the monarch and climbed the same branch.

"I've seen moths before, but none like you."

"My wings are small," said the moth.

"Give them time," said the butterfly, her body still, but her beautiful, delicate wings paddling the air. "Most hang upside-down after the eclose, to let the wings expand and dry. I bet yours are three times that size when they're ready."

The moth dug into the branch and dangled over the edge, her wings pointing to the ground far below. She let the wind blow against them.

Gradually, they emerged.

"Think you can fly now?" said the butterfly.

"I'm not sure," said the moth. "I've never done it before."

"It's easy," said the butterfly. "Flap."

The moth crawled upright to join her new friend on the branch, extended her wings fully, and then batted the air. An erratic flight, but she flew.

"Like that?"

"Like that."

She tried again, landing against the trunk.

"Your wings are loud," said the butterfly, "and you look like a queen bee. I wonder if they'd let you take some. Maybe they wouldn't notice."

"Take what? Notice what?"

"There's honeycomb in a tree in the woods and it's full of honey, which is so much better than nectar, I've heard. I can show you. Maybe you can distract the bees."

"Have you tried honey?"

"Not many butterflies have, if any."

"Wouldn't the bees be mad if we took some, even a little?"

"Just a taste," said the butterfly. "They make too much anyway."

"Just a taste?"

"Follow me, I'll take you there."

The moth fluttered behind the butterfly until they happened upon a honeycomb in a woods buzzing with bees.

On one of the highest branches of a black oak, the honeycomb draped like a blanket.

Hundreds of worker bees covered the surface while others patrolled the air.

The butterfly landed on the branch of a neighboring tree, so the moth joined her.

"It looks dangerous," said the moth.

A few butterfly corpses surrounded the base of the tree.

"Not for you," said the butterfly. "Some of my past friends have tried to get the honey, some stole a taste, but none have returned. You're different, though. Unique, like you said. You look like them. You even smell like them, and your chirping sounds similar to their queen, so you'll fit right in. You have nothing to lose."

"Better than nectar?"

"Better than nectar. One taste and you're hooked."

Hesitating, the moth flew to the honeycomb, landing as far as she could from the bees. They crawled over the nest in waves, around and over each other.

As a caterpillar, she had always relied on her friend for courage. Things were different now that she had transformed. Along with acquiring a new form during the long sleep, she had somehow developed courage, and independence.

The moth with the skull on her back snuck closer, chirping, displaying her bright yellow for all to see.

A single bee crawled toward her, touched her wings, and let her be. Another crawled over her back, but otherwise ignored her, so she crept closer to the masses.

When curious bees approached in droves, she made her noises and they hurried away.

The reluctant moth extended her proboscis into the honey.

From the other tree, the orange monarch butterfly urged her onward. Below: broken butterfly wings and death.

Hundreds of bees watched, some crawling closer to investigate; none seemed threatened by her presence.

They accepted her.

She took a drink—a taste—and the honey filled her with warmth. One drop.

An instant rush.

The butterfly was right.

She thought again of her caterpillar friend, wishing she were around. Perhaps she hadn't survived the attack from the black, eight-legged creature.

Her new friend landed beneath her on the honeycomb.

"Think it's safe?" said the butterfly.

"I don't think so," said the moth. "You should go back."

A few bees flew toward them.

"With you here, it's safe."

"I'll bring you some honey," she said to the butterfly. "Go."

But it was too late.

The moth scurried to her friend and covered her fragile body with her large black wings as the bees descended. One landed next to them, trying to get to the butterfly. Another landed on the moth's back, but her skin was too thick for the stinger to pierce. She screamed, beating her wings against the assault. One sting and either would be dead like those below.

"Just a taste," the moth said to her friend, protecting her.

The butterfly quickly extended her proboscis and tasted the honey.

"Thank you," she said, sliding out from under the cover and fluttering away.

The moth trembled and shook her wings and

batted the bees until they were no longer a threat, until the butterfly was out of harm's way. As they retreated, she smoothed out her wings, embracing her beauty, the black and brown and the yellow. She had truly transformed during holometabolism, and in many ways. Once again she sampled the honey and let the energy surge through her while a white sun warmed her body.

"I have a skull on my back," she said to the world.

THE SCARLET HOURGLASS

1

Everyone knew what the color signified and everyone knew the shape. Red warned of danger, of evil. The shape warned that time would soon be up if crossing her path. The mark blazoned brightly on her stomach, which meant the spider most often kept her back to the world so she wouldn't scare anyone away.

But sometimes she exposed the hourglass proudly, dangling upside-down from her eight black legs.

STAY AWAY, she projected.

The spider didn't have many friends, if any, but she was okay with that. Soon she'd birth her children. Hundreds of them. Hundreds of miniature versions of her and no longer would she be alone.

2

Rain had washed away most of the web she had made the night before. Beads of water glistened on what remained.

She had captured a horsefly and some sort of beetle, planning to eat them this morning, but they were gone, too. They were wrapped in silk blankets to preserve them. The silk blankets were gone. Washed away.

An ache in the spider's belly reminded her that she was hungry. To fend off that hunger, her only choice was to rebuild and start over. She couldn't just go out and look for food. The food had to come to her.

That's the way it worked.

She always felt it was more difficult for widows to find food than other spiders. Although the widow's silk was stronger than all other spiders' silk, this meant her webs were thicker, whiter, more visible to her prey. This meant she ate less often, sometimes not for days, which is why she wrapped her food. She could save it for later if needed.

The only benefit of being able to make stronger webs is that she didn't have to rebuild her webs as often. Yes, the rain had damaged most of her current web, but she could easily build from the structure that remained anchored to the white picket fence and the oak.

Daddy-long-legs and wolf spiders and her other neighbors would have to rebuild from scratch after the lightest of rains. She guessed that's why most of them had started building underneath the overhangs of the house, although even that came with risk.

The humans who dwelled there often took an upturned broom to them, destroying the webs, along with those who built them. The wood pile wasn't a safe place, either, especially during the winter when the chimney smoke plumed.

She felt safe here, by the oak, so she began to rebuild.

3

Time to eat. That's what the hourglass on her stomach told her. Time to hide the scarlet mark and hide her body in the shadows.

A hummingbird with red on its head and back hovered near the web, possibly checking out her handiwork, but her colors warned others to STAY AWAY for as long as the buzz of her wings held her there.

A few pincher bugs skirted the web, as well as a line of black ants and a green bug of some sort, but none were tempted to cross the bridge she had made between the oak tree and the post of the white picket fence.

They could all see her silk.

They could sense the danger.

The spider waited patiently. She lay one of her legs against the silk, waiting for the slightest of vibrations to tell her that a not-so-lucky creature happened upon her trap, but the sun came and went and she stayed hungry.

4

The next day was equally still. Not silent, because there was a lot going on in her environment, but *still*. Not once did her web thrum with good fortune.

A field mouse scurried up the white picket fence. A creature so large would feed her for an un-guessable amount of time, and would feed her children, too, once they found their way into this world. And the spider could take him. That much was certain. One bite and the field mouse would go down. It would go *still*, like the warm afternoon, in a matter of moments.

The web would not hold a field mouse, however. Dumb luck was her only chance. While fast in her youth, old age and a growing body had slowed her down. Ages back, she could have outrun the mouse over a short distance, and ended him quickly.

"I saw your scarlet hourglass from below," said the field mouse, "along with your web. Under the light of the sun, it nearly glows."

The spider ignored him.

She didn't need his mockery or his insults. She needed food and the field mouse—

"And I can see you *now*," he said.

She stepped out from the shadows, if only to let him know she wasn't hiding from him.

"This is what my friends call 'the safe distance'," said the field mouse. "Our kind have seen what your kind can do. Some of our kind have even fallen to your venom."

The widow took a slow step forward. Not moving, but bringing one of her eight legs closer. Then she relaxed, letting the field mouse think she wasn't a threat.

"Plus, I've seen you before. Alone. You are *alone*, aren't you?"

The field mouse looked around cautiously.

"I guess if you had friends, I'd be dead already."

If only he would go and leave her in peace. His presence alone could be scaring away her next meal. If only she were younger, faster, more agile. Yet, she knew how to get rid of him. Mice weren't brave creatures, she knew. They were cowards. All mouth and no bite.

The widow skittered across the web as fast as

she could manage. The field mouse wasn't expecting her to do such a thing and nearly tumbled backwards off the fence. She almost got him, her front-most leg brushing his tail.

The field mouse scurried along the white wood and down the post, hopping to the oak trunk and out of sight. Her empty stomach growled at her for not catching her prey, but the mouse was never prey in her mind, but a nuisance that needed to go. And in that regard, she had succeeded.

The rest of the night was still.

5

In the shadows, the egg sack awaited. The children were starting to grow restless inside. They wanted out, hundreds of them, and when they broke free they would spill out like the seeds of a dropped fig. Hundreds of hungry children looking for food their mother couldn't provide. They would be born into this world, starve, and most likely die, never having had the chance to know what it was like to live.

The widow worked frantically and ceaselessly to expand her web. She fully bridged the gap between the white picket fence and the trunk of the oak. She worked all day and into the night, hungry and starving, but determined to save her children. She would make sure they ate first. She would make sure that they would live. And then, if she had any fight left in her, she'd focus on herself. But first, the children.

6

She was nearly asleep, or perhaps sleeping the long sleep, when something plucked one of the many silk strings.

"What is it?" asked something greenish-yellow and wriggly.

"I don't know," said something yellowish-green and wriggly.

"Looks like a shortcut to me."

They contemplated crossing.

"Let's take the long route," said the yellow.

"It looks strong enough to cross," said the green.

"I think we should continue the way we were going."

"Trust me."

"Come on," said the green. "I'll go first to make sure it's safe."

The green caterpillar stepped onto the silk. She struggled with her footing, but managed to crawl out a ways.

Her back legs stuck to the webbing.

Time was short, so the spider danced across the silk and lunged, her fangs burying deep and fast. She retraced as quickly as she had attacked. It wouldn't take long, but she had always hated this part: the waiting.

The green caterpillar contorted, her body arching and legs kicking, while her companion, a yellow caterpillar with green stripes, inched away in the opposite direction.

She attacked again, not sure if it would make the process go any quicker, but it seemed to have helped.

The yellow caterpillar turned back once more for her friend, so the widow stood upright on her back pairs of legs as a warning.

STAY AWAY, the red hourglass on her belly proclaimed.

The other caterpillar didn't turn around a second time. The spider only ever took what it needed. No one else needed to die.

Working with haste, the widow began spinning her silk, turning the meal for her children round and round within her black needle legs.

7

She counted them, one by one, as they emerged into this world. A hundred ninety-six tiny spiders.

The field mouse stopped by one final time, cautiously.

"Congratulations, miss," he said.

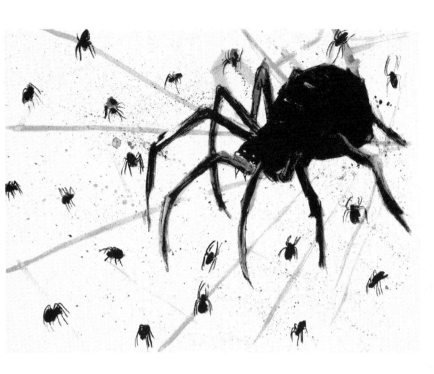

He looked sincere, but looked something else as well, perhaps a shade lighter.

"Looks like me and my family will be moving," he said and disappeared into the night.

No longer alone, the widow counted her children once more and began to rebuild, dangling upside-down on her web, turning over the hourglass.

Made in the USA
Charleston, SC
21 February 2016